For Alison – A.B.
To Debbie and Janetta – M.C.

Text copyright © Antonia Barber 1992, 2014
Illustrations copyright © Margaret Chamberlain 1992, 2014
The rights of Antonia Barber and Margaret Chamberlain to be identified respectively
as the author and illustrator of this work have been asserted by each of them
in accordance with the Copyright, Designs and Patents Act, 1988 (United Kingdom).

First published in Great Britain in 1992 by Frances Lincoln Children's Books,
74-77 White Lion Street, London N1 9PF
www.franceslincoln.com

This edition published 2014

A catalogue record for this book is available from the British Library.

ISBN 978-1-84780-509-6

Printed in China

1 3 5 7 9 8 6 4 2

TALES FROM
GRIMM

Antonia Barber
Margaret Chamberlain

F

FRANCES LINCOLN
CHILDREN'S BOOKS

CONTENTS

TALES FROM GRIMM

The stories known as Grimm's fairy tales were collected by the brothers Jacob and Wilhelm Grimm. Born in Germany in the late 18th century, Jacob and Wilhelm were as close as any two brothers could be, living and working together throughout their lives.

Both were fascinated by folk tales, listening carefully and writing down traditional stories told to them by family, friends, and people from nearby villages and farms.

In 1812 and 1814 they published two volumes of these tales, originally called *Children and Family Stories*. Enormously popular, the tales were soon translated into many languages, and are now famous all over the world.

THE FROG PRINCE

There was once a king, both wise and good, who was blessed with many lovely daughters. The youngest daughter was by far the loveliest and was petted and fussed over by all her sisters. Indeed, she was so beautiful that even the sun in the sky shone more brightly when she was around. This was really rather a nuisance on hot summer days. Then, to escape from the heat, and the fussing of her older sisters, the youngest princess would steal away and play in the cool glades of the old forest that lay just beyond the palace gardens.

The old forest was dim and mysterious and more than a little magical. The princesses had often been warned by their old nurse not to stray into it. But the youngest princess was so much spoilt by her older sisters that she rarely did as she was told.

One tiresomely hot summer day, she was wandering aimlessly in the forest, singing to herself and playing with a golden ball. As always the sun seemed to seek her out, shining down through every gap in the trees.

The princess began to tease the sun, throwing her ball up through the leaves into the bright air. It flashed as the sun caught it, then fell back through the green shadows into the princess's hands. It was fun playing hide and seek with the sun and she laughed, running about on the soft leaves, tossing up the golden ball here and there. Then suddenly the sun found her, shining into her eyes so that she was dazzled and could not see the golden ball as it fell. It slipped through her hands and rolled away towards a still black pool in a deep hollow.

With a cry of dismay the princess ran after it, but it bounced against a twisted

tree root and dropped, with hardly a splash, into the middle of the pool. When she reached the edge of the water, all she could see was a widening ring of dark ripples and a faint gleam of gold vanishing into the depths.

The princess rolled up her silken sleeve and reached her slender arm down into the dark water, but it was too deep. She fetched a dead branch and poked around in the bottom of the pool, but it only made the water muddier. Then she sat down on the bank beside the pool and wept bitterly, for the golden ball had been her favourite plaything.

In a little while, she thought she heard a small voice which said, "King's daughter, why are you weeping?"

The princess opened her eyes and looked around, but seeing no one, went back to her tears.

The voice came again but louder, "King's daughter, what troubles you that you weep so sadly?"

This time the princess brushed away her tears and listened rather fearfully for she remembered her old nurse's warnings. It seemed to her that the voice came from out of the water.

"I'm weeping for my golden ball," she said, "which is lost in the dark pool."

"Dry your tears," said the voice, "for I can help you."

Peering down at the murky water, the princess saw that the voice came from a

small frog which floated beneath the water with only its head showing.

"I can fetch your golden ball," said the frog, "but what will you give me in return?"

"Whatever you ask!" answered the princess in astonishment. "My jewels? My pearls?" She seized the little golden circlet she wore on her head and held it out. "I will give you my crown", she said.

"What use are gold and jewels to me?" asked the frog.

"Tell me what you want then," begged the princess.

"I am lonely here in this dark pool," said the frog sadly. "Give me your company, your friendship . . . perhaps your love?"

The princess stared at the frog's big round eyes and warty skin. My friendship, she thought, my love! For that ugly little frog! But she did so long for her golden ball and, being rather spoilt, was not always honest. She smiled feebly at the frog. "I will be your friend," she said.

"Will you let me sit at table with you?" he asked.

"Yes," said the princess.

"Eat from your plate?"

"Yes."

"Drink from your cup?"

The princess tried not to shudder. "Yes," she said.

"May I sleep on your bed?" asked the frog.

Now the odious creature has gone too far, thought the princess crossly. But since she had no intention of keeping her word, she smiled again and said, "Yes."

"Do you give me your promise?" asked the frog, who did not altogether trust her smile.

The princess crossed her fingers behind her back and said, "I promise."

The frog stared at her for a long moment with his big round eyes. Then with a sudden plop he vanished beneath the water.

The princess waited, holding her breath with excitement, and two minutes later the frog popped up again, clutching the golden ball between his green webbed feet.

Quickly the princess snatched it from him. She washed it clear of the clinging mud and held it up in a shaft of sunlight.

"Thank you, frog," she said. "I must go home now or I shall be late for tea."

"Take me with you," said the frog, clambering out of the pool.

"Why, you must follow me as best you can," said the princess, and she ran off as fast as her legs could carry her. When she reached the palace gardens she was out of breath, but she had left the frog far behind.

"Well I shan't see him again!" she said.

But on the following day, when the king and his family sat dining with all the court, the frog reached the palace and made his way, one hop at a time, up the wide staircase. He was hungry and very tired and when he reached the door of the great hall, he knocked and called, "King's daughter, open the door to me!"

Now the youngest princess had quite forgotten about the frog, never dreaming that he would follow her so far. She went to the door and opened it. She glanced about but at first could see no one until a voice at her feet said, "King's daughter, let me come in and dine with you."

The princess was horrified. She slammed the door shut and stood with her back against the lock.

The king, seeing his daughter's wide eyes and open mouth, smiled at her dismay. "Who is there, daughter?" he called. "Is it some giant come to carry you away?"

The room grew silent as everyone turned to stare at the youngest princess.

She hung her head. "No, father," she said in a small voice. "It is only a frog."

At this a great roar of laughter ran round the table and the princess wished that the ground would swallow her.

"A talking frog?" exclaimed the king. "Why, this will amuse us all. Pray bid him come in."

"But, father," said the princess, "you don't understand. He wants to sit by me and eat from my plate."

"Does he, indeed!" exclaimed the king. "And by what right does he claim to dine with my daughter?" The princess saw that the truth could not be hidden. She was forced to tell her father, in front of everyone, how the frog had found her golden ball and of the promises she had given.

The king no longer smiled but listened with a solemn face. When she had finished, he sat a while in silence while the courtiers whispered among themselves. Then he said thoughtfully: "A talking frog. . . and in the old forest. . ."

Now I have told you that he was wise as well as just and he knew something of the magic of the old forest. Suddenly he smiled and seemed to make up his mind.

"Let the frog come in," he said.

"But, father. . . !" wailed the youngest princess.

"No 'buts'!" said the king. "You gave him your word and you must keep it!"

The princess bit her lip angrily, but she knew better than to argue with her father. She opened the door the merest crack, then ran back to her chair and sat down. She stared hard at the tablecloth in front of her while all other eyes turned towards the door.

In came the frog, hopping wearily across the cold marble floor until he reached the princess's chair. "Lift me up, king's daughter," he said, "that I may eat from your plate."

The princess would not look at him. She glanced desperately at her father who said nothing but nodded sternly. With a sigh, the princess picked up the frog and put it on the table. It hopped across and sat beside her golden plate.

"Welcome, frog," said the king. "We thank you for your kindness to our daughter. Feed and drink with us to your heart's content."

To everyone's astonishment, the frog rose up on his hind legs and bowed politely, though not very elegantly. Then he sat down again and helped himself to food from the princess's plate. A burst of conversation began again and everyone wanted to talk to the frog. He proved himself courteous and witty and, as some of the ladies remarked, "really rather charming".

Only the youngest princess remained uncharmed, sulking gloomily and picking at her food.

Now, the frog had made a long journey for so small a creature. As the meal ended, his wide mouth stifled a yawn and his goggle eyes grew sleepy.

"I think," said the king kindly, "that we should not keep our guest from his sleep."

"Indeed," said the frog, "I shall be grateful to lie down if the princess will be kind enough to carry me to her room."

It was too much for the princess. "I am not having that frog in my bedroom!" she shouted, quite forgetting her good manners.

But her father was adamant. "The frog is courteous," he said, "and more fitted to be a king's son, by his manners, than you are to be a king's daughter."

"If his father is a king, he is a fat, frog king," said the princess rudely, "and no frog prince is sleeping in my bed!"

Then the king saw how badly his youngest daughter had been spoilt, and he resolved that she should learn her lesson. "The frog helped you when you were in trouble," he said gravely, "and you must not now despise him. He shall sleep this night on your pillow as you promised him."

When the princess began to protest again he added: "If you do not choose to sleep in your bed tonight, there is always the palace dungeon!"

The youngest princess knew that her father meant what he said. She pursed her lips, picked up the frog between two fingers and holding him at arm's length, stamped off up the palace stairs. When she reached her room she dropped him disdainfully in the darkest corner and tried to pretend he was not there.

But when she climbed into bed, the frog came hopping across the room and called: "Lift me on to your pillow, king's daughter, for I am weary and cannot jump so far."

The princess looked at him thoughtfully. Now that they were away from the laughing courtiers, she did not mind him so much. He was friendly and funny, he did not fuss as her sisters did, and not many princesses had a talking frog for a friend.

"If I lift you up on to my pillow," she asked, "will you tell me a story?"

"With pleasure," said the frog. "I am very good at stories."

So the princess lifted him up and then, tired out after her tantrums, she put her head down on her pillow and closed her eyes. And the little frog sat on the corner of her pillow and told her a long story which was exciting, and sad, and funny, and all the things a good story should be. As he told the story he drew closer and closer until, at the end, he sat beside her sleepy head.

The princess gave a contented sigh. "That was the best story ever, frog," she said. Through drooping eyelids she saw his friendly face and goggle eyes close to her own and found to her surprise that she rather liked them. "Goodnight, frog," she said, and she gave him a small peck of a kiss on the side of his funny green head.

What happened next had her leaping out of bed in astonishment. There was a blinding flash of light, a huge puff of smoke and a noise like a clap of thunder, And there, where the little green frog had been, was the most handsome prince the king's daughter had ever seen. His eyes were kind and beautiful, if a little

dazed, and he seemed rather embarrassed to find himself sitting on the princess's pillow.

The noise brought the king, the courtiers and all the princess's sisters running upstairs, and the prince explained to them all how he had been bewitched many years before by a particularly nasty witch. He had fallen foul of her when only a boy and had spent many weary years seeking a princess who would kiss him and break the spell.

Everyone was amazed at his story except the wise king, who had rather suspected something of the sort. "After all," he told them, "it's not every day you meet a frog who can talk."

Of course, the prince and princess fell deeply in love with each other. In due time they were married and lived together happily ever after. And if the youngest princess sometimes called her beloved husband "Frogface", she only did it when they were alone together.

HANSEL AND GRETEL

At the edge of a great forest, a poor woodcutter lived with his wife and his two children. The boy was named Hansel and the girl Gretel and their mother had died when they were very young. Their father's new wife did not care for her two stepchildren, indeed she begrudged them the very food that went into their mouths.

One day there came a great famine upon the land and the poor woodcutter could find no food for his little family.

"We can no longer feed the children," said his wife at last. "We have barely enough for ourselves. If you do not eat, husband, you cannot work and then we shall be penniless. Let us take the children into the forest and leave them to feed on roots and berries as best they may."

At first the woodcutter would not listen to her, but she gave him no peace. "Unless the children go, we shall all starve," she told him, "and where is the sense in that?"

The woodcutter knew in his heart that she was wrong, but he had not the strength to hold out against her. He agreed that, on the morrow, they should do as she said.

Hansel and Gretel, lying awake in their hunger, heard all that was said. Gretel began to weep silently, but Hansel rose up and stole quietly out into the garden. There he gathered up the white pebbles that shone like silver coins in the moonlight. He filled his pockets with them and went back into the house. "Sleep in peace, little sister," he said. "God will not forsake us."

"Rise up," called the stepmother in the morning. "We are going to gather wood in the forest." She gave each child a scrap of bread saying, "Make it last, for there will be nothing more to eat today."

They all went out into the forest and as they went, Hansel turned back every little while towards the house.

"Why do you lag behind us?" called his father.

"I am looking at my little white cat on the roof of the house," said Hansel. "It is saying goodbye to me."

"Fool!" said his stepmother crossly. "It is only the morning sun upon the white chimney."

But in truth, Hansel turned back to drop the white stones that would mark his way home.

In a clearing deep in the forest, the woodcutter built a fire.

"Rest here, and eat your bread," said the stepmother. "When your father and I have gathered enough wood, we will return for you."

Hansel and Gretel sat beside the fire, eating their bread crumb by crumb, and took comfort from the sound of their father's axe as he worked in the distance. But the sound was no more than an old branch, blown by the wind against a dead tree.

In time the children fell asleep, and did not wake until night came. The fire burned low and the children grew cold. Gretel was afraid but Hansel said, "Wait until the moon shines and we will find our way home." They clung together shivering until at last the moon rose, cold and bright, above the tree tops, picking out the white pebbles along the pathway.

"Come," said Hansel and taking Gretel by the hand, led her through the forest. All night they walked, and by dawn came safely to their father's door.

Their stepmother was angry when she saw them returning, but she hid her anger. "Why did you wander off into the forest, you bad children," she said. "We feared that you would never return." Only their father was truly pleased to see them, for his conscience had troubled him.

All went well until the next year when there was an even worse famine. Again the woodcutter was in despair, and again his wife argued that they should lose the children in the forest. "We will take them further this time," she said, "so that they will not return."

"No!" said the woodcutter. "I cannot do it. Better that we should share our last crust with our children."

But again his wife gave him no peace, saying that if the children did not take their chance in the forest, they would all starve to death. And at last the woodcutter allowed himself to be persuaded.

Once again, the children overheard the conversation and Hansel rose up in the night to fetch pebbles from the garden. But this time the stepmother had locked the door and Hansel could not get out.

"What shall we do?" asked Gretel.

"Go to sleep, little sister," said Hansel. "God will provide."

Next day, before they set out into the forest, Hansel broke up his piece of bread in his pocket.

"Why are you lagging behind, Hansel?" called his father as the boy paused and turned back yet again.

"I am saying goodbye to the white pigeon which sits on the roof," said Hansel.

"Fool!" said his stepmother. "It is only the sun on the white chimney."

But Hansel was scattering the little white crumbs of bread so that they would mark out the path.

Once more the children were left beside a fire in the forest, and when the moon rose they set out a second time to find their way home. But they saw that the birds had picked up every white crumb Hansel had scattered, and they knew that they were lost indeed.

For three long days they wandered through the trackless forest, with nothing to eat but a few sour berries which the birds had missed. Each night they huddled together for warmth, for they had no flint to light a fire. There were racked with pains of hunger, and weary from their hopeless wandering.

Then, finding their way into a sunlit clearing, they saw before them a strange little house. It seemed to be made all of gingerbread with flat cakes like tiles upon the roof and clear panes of sugar for the windows. There was no one to be seen and Hansel and Gretel were so hungry, they set about the house without a second thought, breaking pieces from the roof and licking holes in the sugar panes.

Soon they grew even bolder. Hansel pulled off a whole tile, and Gretel broke a piece out of the window-pane, and they sat down against the wall of the house to enjoy their spoils. But at that moment the door of the house creaked slowly open, and a very bent, very ugly old woman came out.

At first Hansel and Gretel were very much afraid. But the old woman smiled, showing broken teeth, and said, "Come into my little house, children, and stay with me. I will do you no harm." They could hardly believe their good fortune as she took them by the hand and led them into the gingerbread house. She gave them apples and milk to drink. She gave them nuts and made them pancakes.

And when they had eaten their fill, she led them to two little beds which smelled sweetly of fresh linen, and there settled them down to sleep.

Now the old woman was really a cruel witch who ate little children. She had built the gingerbread house only to tempt them into her clutches. She looked down at the two children, who were soon lying fast asleep, and thought, I will eat the boy first. She picked Hansel up and carried him while he slept to a little shed with iron bars. As she locked him in, Hansel woke up and began to kick and scream, but the witch only laughed.

She woke Gretel and said, "Fetch water and cook food to feed up your brother, for I mean to eat him when he is fat enough."

Poor Gretel was terrified; she wept and pleaded but it was no use. She could not free poor Hansel and she would not leave him, so she was forced to do as the witch said.

Weeks passed while Hansel was given all the best food and Gretel had only the scraps. Each morning the old witch would tell Hansel to poke out a finger through the bars, so that she could feel how fat he was getting. It was fortunate that, like all witches, she had very weak eyes by daylight. So Hansel held out an old rabbit bone to her and the witch, believing it to be his finger, marvelled that he did not grow fatter.

At last she resolved to eat Gretel first instead and thought of a way to trick her. "We will bake today," she told the girl. "Heat up the oven while I make the dough." When the dough was ready she said, "Look into the oven, girl, and see if it is hot enough."

The witch planned to push Gretel into the oven and close the door. But Gretel was too clever for her. "How am I to look inside?" she asked. "The door is much too small."

"Nonsense!" said the witch crossly. "The door is quite big enough, you foolish girl. See, even I can get my head inside."

So saying, she opened the oven door and peered inside herself. At once Gretel pushed her with all her might and slammed shut the iron door behind her. There was a terrible howl, then a great flash and the witch was gone, for witches cannot stand the fire.

"The witch is dead! She is dead!" cried Gretel, running to free Hansel from his prison. Out he flew like a bird from its cage and the two children hugged each other and shed tears of joy.

Now that the witch was gone, the two children went back into her house and found chests of jewels and pearls. Hansel filled his pockets and Gretel her apron. Then, breaking off pieces of the house to give them food for the journey, they set out in search of their home.

They walked for many hours through the dark forest, until in time it grew lighter and the sun shone through. After a while it seemed to them that the path they followed was somehow familiar. They hurried on and, at last, saw their father's house in the clearing ahead.

Now, after they had abandoned the children in the forest, nothing had gone well with the woodcutter and his wife. The stepmother grew sick and soon died, while the father lived on alone, mourning for his lost children. When he saw Hansel and Gretel coming towards him along the forest path, the poor man could hardly believe his eyes. He ran weeping to meet them and gathered them both into his arms. Gretel tipped out from her apron the jewels she had found in the witch's house and Hansel emptied his pockets. Then the woodcutter saw with joy that in all their days they need never go hungry again.

BRIAR-ROSE

There lived long ago a king and queen who had waited many years for a child. At last, when they had almost given up hope, the queen gave birth to a beautiful baby girl.

The king was delighted and ordered that a great feast should be held to celebrate his daughter's christening. He invited to the palace his relations, his friends and everyone of any importance in the land.

"I shall invite all the wise women in my kingdom to act as the princess's godmothers," he told the queen, "They will give her gifts that money cannot buy."

The royal chamberlain frowned when he heard this and pointed out to the king that there were thirteen wise women in the land.

"Thirteen is an unlucky number," he said. "It would be most unsuitable."

"Well, choose the best twelve," said the king impatiently, for he was busy fussing over all the arrangements for the grand banquet. He thought that one godmother more or less made little difference; but he was wrong.

The christening feast was the most splendid that had ever been held in that land and, when it was over, the twelve wise women came forward in turn to bestow their magic gifts upon the baby princess.

The first wise woman gave her goodness, the second beauty; the third, riches and the fourth, good health. The fifth gave her the gift of laugher; the sixth, a loving heart; the seventh gave her courage and the eighth, gentleness. The ninth gave her a sweet singing voice and the tenth, not to be outdone, added dancing feet. The eleventh wise woman gave her skilful hands and the twelfth was just trying to think of anything that was left, when into the great hall stormed the thirteenth wise woman. She was disagreeable at the best of times and now she was in a great rage at the insult of being left out.

"I will give your pretty darling something to look forward to," she cried, shaking her fist in the king's face. "At the end of her fifteenth year, she shall prick her finger upon a spindle and fall down dead!" So saying, she gave a great cackle of laughter and, swirling her great, dark cloak about her, swept out down the marble steps of the palace.

When she had gone, there was a terrible silence. The guests stood frozen with horror; the king turned very pale, and the queen burst into a flood of tears. The king turned to the twelfth wise woman, who had still to give her gift, and begged her to undo the other's magic.

"That I cannot," she said sadly, "for her power is as great as mine. But I will do what I can. Though it shall come about as she said, yet the princess shall not die, but shall fall into a deep sleep which shall last for a hundred years. In all that time, she shall not age, nor suffer any harm, but shall wake at last as if from her night's rest."

Then the queen cried out, "I beseech you, let me sleep with my child, lest she wake to find herself motherless and alone."

"Why, it shall be so," said the twelfth wise woman gently. "When the princess sleeps, so shall you all!"

The young princess grew up with all the gifts that had been wished upon her. She was beautiful and kind and brave and gentle. When her people heard her sweet voice, or watched her dancing, their hearts were filled with joy, and the sound of her laughter brightened their days. As for her hands, they were as skilful as any in the kingdom except in one thing: for she could not spin. While she was still in her cradle the king had given orders that every spindle in the land should be burnt,

and the people had obeyed him willingly. For in every sharp spindle they saw a terrible threat to their beloved princess, and they hoped, by their care, that she might escape the thirteenth wise woman's curse.

On the day of the princess's fifteenth birthday, the whole palace was busy with preparations for a great party. The royal chamberlain, the ladies-in-waiting, the maids and the footmen were all hurrying about their duties. Down below in the royal kitchen, meat was roasting, pies were baking, cakes were being decorated, and everything was in great confusion.

The princess, seeking a little peace and quietness, slipped away to the oldest part of the palace which was seldom used. Climbing the winding stair of a higher tower, she came upon a tiny room locked with a rusty key. She turned the key, which creaked in the lock, and pushed open the heavy door. Inside the room sat an old woman with a spindle, busily spinning flax.

The princess had never seen a spindle before and she watched in fascination as it whirled around. Greeting the old woman politely, she asked what she was doing.

"Why, I am spinning thread, my pretty," said the old woman smiling. "Would you like to try your hand at it?"

The princess was delighted and reached out to take the spindle but, as she did so, she fell under the power of the magic curse. She cried out as the point of the spindle pricked her finger, and at once she grew dizzy and could not stand. There was an old bed in one corner of the room and she sat down on it as a great tiredness overwhelmed her. The sound of the old woman laughing seemed to fade upon the air, and a moment later the princess was asleep.

And at that very moment, throughout the whole castle, everyone else began to fall asleep too. The king slumped suddenly sideways on his throne with his crown tilted over one eye; the queen tried to hide a little yawn behind her white hand, but the hand fell to her lap and lay motionless.

The royal chamberlain, striding importantly down a long corridor, grew suddenly weak at the knees and, sitting down upon a velvet chair, was soon snoring noisily. The maids-in-waiting gave little cries of dismay and sank down like flowers amid the wide skirts of their silken dresses.

In the kitchen, the cook was scolding the scullery boy and threatening him with her wooden spoon. But the spoon dropped from her hand as she fell against the table, overturning a big bowl of custard. The kitchen cat, unable to believe her good fortune, ran forward from under the table to lick up the golden sweetness; but before she had lapped twice, she too was lying still beside the yellow pool.

Soon, where all had been confusion, there was no sound but the crackle of the fire and the slow drip of custard. Then the very flame grew still and the spilt custard hung from the table like a yellow icicle.

Outside, the horses slept in their stables, and the hounds in their kennels. The doves slept on the palace roofs with their heads beneath their wings; even the very leaves on the trees hung motionless in the palace gardens.

But in the forest beyond the garden, all was movement as the briars began to grow. Up between the trees, higher and higher, backwards and forwards they twisted and turned, weaving a hedge of fierce thorns and sweet roses so that none should pass into the enchanted palace. At last nothing could be seen, not even the silken standard on the topmost tower.

Years passed, and the story of the beautiful princess who slept behind the forest of briars grew into legend. Some people held that it was true, others that it was no more than a fairy tale, told to while away a winter's night. From time to time princes would come from far-off lands, drawn by word of the great beauty of Princess Briar-Rose (for so they called her) who slept in the hidden palace. But none could pass through the forest of briars, for the sharp thorns caught them and held them and they were lucky if they escaped with their lives.

Many long years went by and then at last a certain king's son who was travelling through the land chanced to spend the night at an inn close by. When darkness fell and stories were told around the fire, an old man recalled the legend of Princess Briar-Rose, who slept with all her father's court in the depths of the forest. He was a good story-teller and as he spoke of the princess's great beauty, and the mysterious enchanted palace, the prince gazed into the dying fire and seemed to see it all.

"Here's gold for your story," he said when the tale was done, "for you told it as if it were true."

"Why, so it is, my lord," said the old man. "I heard it from my own grandfather and he saw the princess with his own eyes, when he was but a young man."

"Tell me, then, where I may find this palace," said the prince eagerly, "for I shall not rest until I see Briar-Rose for myself."

"It is useless," said the old man. "None can pass into that enchanted place."

But the prince would not heed him, and set out alone deep into the forest.

By now, it happened that the hundred years of the enchantment drew to a close and the day came when the princess would wake again. When the prince reached the briar hedge, all the thorns were gone. Only the sweet-scented roses covered the briars, which parted before him and closed again when he had passed. When he reached the palace everything stood as the old man had said: the horses slept in the stables, the hounds in their kennels, and the birds upon the rooftops.

The prince went in through the kitchen door, where the cat slept beside the custard, and the cook beside the scullery boy. He walked up the marble stairs and along the corridor, where the lord chamberlain snored on a velvet chair. He passed into the great room where the ladies-in-waiting lay scattered like flowers across the carpet, and the king and queen slept upon their thrones. But nowhere could he see Princess Briar-Rose.

He searched without success through all the castle until, at last, he came upon the winding stair that led to the highest tower. There, at the top, he found the little room where Briar-Rose lay sleeping. She was so beautiful that once he had gazed upon her, he could not look away. Gently he stooped and kissed her, and at that very moment the hundred years ended. Princess Briar-Rose opened her eyes and smiled at him.

Then the prince took her by the hand and they went down together, and as Briar-Rose passed through the palace, the long spell was broken.

The king sat up on his throne and straightened his crown. The queen woke with a start and wondered if anyone had noticed that she was yawning. The lord chamberlain rose from his velvet chair, trying to remember what important business he had been attending to; the ladies-in-waiting scrambled hastily to their feet, brushing the creases out of their silken skirts.

In the kitchen the fire crackled, the custard dripped, and the cat went on lapping. The cook rose up from the floor and, before the scullery boy could gather his wits, beat him with her wooden spoon for spilling the custard. Soon all was confusion again, and Princess Briar-Rose laughed with delight as she passed on into the gardens. The birds woke up and flew off into the trees, which seemed to rustle their leaves in welcome. The horses neighed in the stables, the hounds barked in the kennels and everything was just as it had been before. Indeed, the prince had some difficulty in persuading them all that they had, in truth, slept for a hundred years, and that the curse which they had feared for so long was already over.

Now the princess's birthday was celebrated with even greater joy (though Briar-Rose was a little uncertain whether she was fifteen or a hundred and fifteen). In due time, she was married to her prince and they lived together in contentment to the end of their days.

RAPUNZEL

In a far land, there once lived a husband and wife who for many years had longed for a child. And then, at last, it seemed that their prayers would be answered.

Now it often happens that a woman with child has a great craving for some special food, and this wife was no exception. The windows at the back of their house looked down upon a beautiful garden full of herbs and flowers. One in particular, which in that land is called rapunzel, looked so green and delicious that the wife felt that she could not live without tasting it.

When she told her husband he turned pale with fear, for the garden belonged to a powerful enchantress and none dared set foot in it.

As the days passed, the wife's craving grew even stronger and she began to pine and grow weak. When he saw this, the husband decided that he would rather risk his own life than lose his wife and the hope of a child. So he climbed swiftly down over the wall and, without being seen, gathered a bunch of the green herb and took it back to his wife. She devoured it eagerly, as if she could never have enough, and the next day craved it more than ever. Once more her husband ventured down into the garden, but this time he was not so fortunate. As he turned with his hands full of the green rapunzel, he found himself face to face with the enchantress.

When she saw that he had not only trespassed in her garden, but had stolen some of her herbs, her anger was very terrible. "For this," she said, "you must surely die!"

The husband did not want to die, leaving his wife alone and his child fatherless. He pleaded with the enchantress, telling her of the coming child and of his wife's great craving for the rapunzel. Now the enchantress, for all her power, was often lonely.

When she heard of the child, she smiled.

"Then I will spare you," she said, "and let you take all the herbs your wife desires." Still trembling with fear, the husband could scarcely believe his good fortune until she added, "But when the child is born, you must give it to me."

The husband pleaded, but she would not change her mind: he must either die or give up the child.

The enchantress promised that she would care for the child as if it were her own and at last the husband consented.

When the wife learned what had happened, she wept bitterly; but she loved her husband and dreaded to lose him.

The baby was a little girl and very beautiful. Soon after she was born, the enchantress came and took her away to her own splendid house. She named her Rapunzel and brought her up with every luxury that riches could provide. As for her parents, they had to be content with glimpsing her sometimes as she played in the garden.

The child was not unhappy for she had known no other life and could not remember her parents. All went well with her until she began to grow up. With each year she grew lovelier and the enchantress became afraid that some young man would come and steal her treasure away. Young girls are foolish, she thought, and fall in love with the first handsome face they see.

So the enchantress used her magic powers to build a tall tower, deep in the mountain forests, and there she hid Rapunzel away.

Now in this tower there was no door nor any stairway but at the top was a large and splendid room with a small window. No one could get in and Rapunzel could not get out. When the enchantress came to visit her, she would call up to the window, "Rapunzel, Rapunzel, let down your golden hair."

Rapunzel's hair was her greatest beauty: it was fine and golden and very, very long.

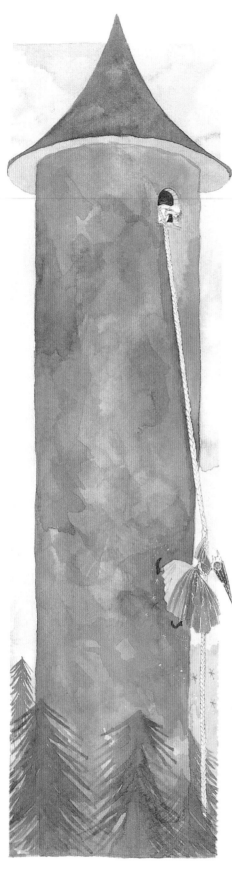

When she heard the enchantress call, she would loosen the long braids of her hair, twist them around the hooks of the window shutters and drop the ends out of the window where they reached right to the ground. Then the enchantress would use the braids like a rope to climb up to the window.

Years passed, and so remote was the tower, that no other living soul passed by. Rapunzel came to believe that she and the enchantress were the only people in all the world.

Then, one day, a king's son lost his way in the forest and heard in its green depths a clear voice singing. Drawn by the gentle beauty of the sound, he came to the tower and, peering up through the trees, saw Rapunzel at her high window. He searched for a door to enter the tower, but could find none on any side. As he stood in the shadows, listening to the sweet singing, the enchantress arrived and called to Rapunzel, who at once let down her golden hair.

As she looked out from the high window, the prince saw clearly her lovely face and longed to speak to her. When at last he saw the enchantress climb down in the same way that she had climbed up, he knew that there was no other way to enter the tower. So he waited until night fell and then approached the tower cautiously. A golden light shone from the high window on to the surrounding darkness, and the soft sound of Rapunzel's singing drifted upon the night air.

Then the prince called softly, "Rapunzel, Rapunzel, let down your golden hair," At once the beautiful hair was uncoiled and the king's son climbed up.

Rapunzel had never seen a young man before and was, at first, very frightened. But the prince talked to her gently, soothing away her fears and winning her trust and love. He told her how he had been entranced by her singing and moved with love by the sight of her sweet face. He begged to be allowed to visit her again and at last she agreed.

So while the enchantress visited Rapunzel each day, the prince, unbeknown to her, would come when darkness fell. Soon Rapunzel and the young prince were deeply in love: he asked her to marry him and return with him to his father's kingdom. Rapunzel was willing but could not see how she could escape from the tower. "I shall have to cut off all my hair," she said, "if I am to climb down myself."

The prince could not bear to think of his lovely bride shorn of her wondrous hair. He proposed that he should bring with him each time he came a skein of silk and that, little by little, Rapunzel should weave a rope by which they might both climb down. So each night the prince brought a new skein, and each day Rapunzel wove the rope a little longer, but always before the enchantress came, she hid it inside one of her silken cushions.

But lovers carry the thought of each other so much in mind that it is hard to keep from speaking the beloved's name. One day as Rapunzel waited patiently while the enchantress climbed up her braided hair, she sighed and murmured, "How slow she is compared to my sweet prince, for he is with me in a moment."

The enchantress had ears as keen as a bat's and she caught the soft sigh. "What!" she cried. "Have you deceived me in spite of all my care?! Then she seized Rapunzel in anger and so terrified her that she confessed all.

When the enchantress learned of the prince's visits and of their plans to escape from the tower, her rage was fearful to behold. She took hold of Rapunzel's hair and, snatching up a pair of scissors, hacked at the shining braids, until Rapunzel's head was jagged and shorn and the hair lay like a pool of gold upon the floor. Then she carried poor Rapunzel far away by her magic into a trackless desert and left her there to survive as best she might.

Even this cruelty did not satisfy her fierce rage against the prince who had planned to steal her treasure. When darkness fell, she tied the golden braids to the shutter hook and waited in the darkness like a spider in a dark crevice.

The prince reached the tower and, seeing the golden braids, climbed swiftly up, eager to greet his love. As he reached the window, the enchantress rushed at him with a terrible shriek.

"Did you think to steal my bird from her nest?" she cried. "Well, she is flown, and the cat shall have your eyes!" And so saying she flew at him with her long fingernails. The prince leaped backwards to escape her claws and fell headlong from the high tower. Then by her magic, the enchantress caused briars with huge thorns to grow below so that the prince fell among them and was blinded. Now his plight was sad indeed: sightless he roamed through the dark forest, living as best he could on berries and roots and mourning always for the loss of his dear love.

But love is more powerful than hatred. Always, as the prince stumbled through the dark forest, and Rapunzel wandered in the trackless desert, some magic drew each towards the other. After many years the prince, as he wandered, heard a faint voice singing and the sound awakened old memories. It seemed to him that he heard Rapunzel's voice and, unable to see, he stretched out his hands and called her name.

Rapunzel looked up and saw him coming and at the sight of his blind eyes, she wept and folded her arms around him. Then two of the tears which ran down her cheeks fell into his sightless eyes, and at once the prince found that he could see again. Words cannot describe their joy as each gazed upon the other's face, and the tears they shed then were tears of purest happiness.

The prince took Rapunzel back to his father's kingdom, where they were married amid great rejoicing, and they lived out their days in peace and happiness.

LITTLE RED-CAP

Once upon a time there lived a little girl who was loved by all who knew her. But the one who love her most was her old grandmother who lived in a cottage in the forest nearby. The old woman liked to make clothes for her little granddaughter and once gave her a little cap of red velvet. The child was so delighted with this gift that she wore it all the time and the people round about called her "Little Red-Cap".

Little Red-Cap would often spend the night with her grandmother and one spring day she set out for the house in the forest. Her mother put some cake and a bottle of wine into a little basket.

"Your grandmother has not been well," she told Little Red-Cap, "and these will tempt her to eat again. Keep to the path or you may trip over some brambles and break the bottle."

The child promised to be careful and set off, singing cheerfully to herself, into the sunlit woodland. But a little way along the path she met a wolf.

Now this wolf was very wicked and, indeed, was on his way to eat up the old grandmother. He had heard that she was weak and ill and thought that she would not be able to escape him. But when he saw the little girl, looking so plump and delicious beneath her red velvet cap, he decided that she would be a tastier morsel.

"Good morning, Little Red-Cap," said the wolf. "Where are you off to this fine spring day?"

"I am taking some cake and wine to my grandmother," said Little Red-Cap. "She is not well and it will help to make her strong again."

"How very kind!" said the wolf, walking along beside her. He was trying to work out a plan to catch her, for he was an old wolf and thought that she might outrun him if he gave chase. I will hide in the old woman's cottage, he thought cunningly, and trap Little Red-Cap there. I must find some way to reach the house before her.

The path wound through a clearing where flowers danced beneath the budding trees.

"How beautiful!" exclaimed the wolf. "The sight of such lovely flowers would surely cheer the heart of your poor grandmother."

"That is true," said Little Red-Cap, hesitating, "but my mother told me not to stray from the path."

"What harm can it do to stray a little way," said the wolf, "if the flowers give pleasure to a sick old woman?"

"Perhaps you are right," said Little Red-Cap and, putting her basket safely at the foot of a tree, she left the path and began to gather the flowers.

"Well, I must be on my way," said the wolf, and once out of sight he ran as swiftly as he could to the grandmother's cottage.

The door was unlatched for the old woman was expecting her dear grandchild. The wolf burst in, terrifying the old lady who screamed and fainted away at the sight of him. The wolf wondered whether to gobble her up first, but she looked very thin and bony. Little Red-Cap was a much more tempting dish, he decided, and she might arrive at any moment.

He opened the clothes chest at the foot of the bed, pulled out a nightdress and a lace cap, then bundled the old woman inside and closed the lid. He put on the nightdress and cap, leapt into bed and had just settled himself comfortably when the door opened and Little Red-Cap came in.

The moment she came through the door, Little Red-Cap sensed that there was something wrong. There was a rank smell in the air and her grandmother, who lay with her nightcap pulled low over her eyes, looked very strange.

So she did not run up as usual to kiss her grandmother but stood hesitating in the doorway.

"Come closer, my dear," said the wolf in a squeaky voice. "Give your old grandmother a kiss."

Little Red-Cap came a little closer. "Oh, grandmother," she said. "What big ears you have!"

"All the better to hear you with, my child," said the wolf, staring at her.

Little Red-Cap took another step towards the bed. "But, grandmother, what big eyes you have!" she said.

"All the better to see you with, my dear," said the wolf and beckoned her to come closer.

Little Red-Cap looked at the wolf's paws. "Why, grandmother," she said. "What big hands you have!"

"All the better to hug you with, my pretty," said the wolf and tried an encouraging smile.

"Oh, grandmother," said Little Red-Cap, staring in horror at the sharp teeth. "What a big mouth you have!"

The wolf saw that she was not deceived. "All the better to eat you with!" he cried and sprang out of bed with a terrible roar.

If Little Red-Cap had been one step closer, she would have been lost. As it was she fled shrieking through the open door, just as a hunter passed on his way through the forest. When he saw the wolf, the hunter raised his gun to his shoulder.

"No, no!" cried Little Red-Cap. "I think he has eaten my grandmother and if you shoot you may kill her too."

The huntsman lowered his gun and the wolf escaped into the forest.

Little Red-Cap and the hunter went back into the house and heard muffled groans coming from the clothes chest. They opened it up and found the poor

grandmother who could scarcely breathe.

"I should have killed the wolf," said the hunter. "I fear he may return. Bolt the door, Little Red-Cap, and fasten the shutters before you sleep tonight."

The hunter went on his way and Little Red-Cap bolted the door and shuttered the windows. She put her old grandmother back to bed and fed her on cake and wine until she felt a little stronger.

From time to time, Little Red-Cap peeped out through the holes in the shutters, to see if there was any sign of the wolf, but always the forest seemed quiet and peaceful. But at last night fell and then Little Red-Cap felt afraid, for she could not tell what lurked in the darkness outside.

As she sat in the candlelight beside her grandmother's bed, she heard someone scraping at the lock. He will not get in through the door, thought Little Red-Cap.

Then she heard a scrabbling at the shutters. He will not get in through the windows either, she thought.

Then she heard a scurrying on the roof above her and a piece of broken tile fell clattering into the grate. "Oh, grandmother," said Little Red-Cap. "What if the wolf comes down the chimney?"

"Set a light to the fire, my dear," said her grandmother, "and swing the great cooking pot over it."

Little Red-Cap did as her grandmother said, and soon the fire took hold and the great cooking pot began to murmur.

"Take off the lid," said the old lady, "I was boiling sausages yesterday and the smell of the sausage water will tempt him."

Little Red-Cap took off the lid and the smell of sausages rose up the wide chimney.

Now the wolf was very hungry by this time. He had planned to climb carefully down inside the chimney and to eat up Little Red-Cap and her grandmother. But the smell of the sausage water was too much for him.

He sniffed and stretched out his neck: then he sniffed again, leaning further and further over the top of the chimney. Suddenly, his claws slipped on the tiles and over he went, plunging headlong down the chimney. He landed in the great cooking pot with a terrible howl. In a flash, Little Red-Cap popped on the lid and held it shut until the wolf was drowned.

And from that day Little Red-Cap lived happily and went often through the forest to visit her grandmother, but was never troubled by wolves again.

THE GOLDEN GOOSE

Long ago in a far land there were three brothers. The older two were handsome and clever and their parents thought the world of them. The youngest son was plain and simple and was scorned by both his parents and his brothers. His name was Walter but his family called him Wally.

One morning the father sent his eldest son into the forest to cut wood for the fire. His mother fussed over him, packing a little basket with cherry cake and sweet wine so that he should lack nothing for his comfort while he worked.

As he went through the forest, the eldest son met an old man who said, "Kind sir, I am hungry. Can you spare me a little food?"

"Why, I have only a piece of cherry cake and a little sweet wine," said the eldest son. "If I give you some, there will not be enough for me." And with that he passed by and left the old man staring after him. But when the eldest son began to cut down a tree, the axe struck a glancing blow and cut him on the arm.

When he saw that he was wounded, he set up a great wailing and hurried home to his mother, who bound up his arm and put him to bed where she could watch over him.

Then the father sent his second son into the forest to cut wood and again his mother packed a basket with cherry cake and sweet wine.

The second son also met with the old man who said, "Sweet master, spare me a little food for it is a long time since I have eaten."

"I have not eaten myself since breakfast time," said the second son, "and I don't have enough for two." And without pausing he went on into the forest, while the old man stared after him.

When the second son came to cut down a tree, the axe slipped again and cut him on the leg. Home he went in great distress and his mother bound up his leg and put him to bed beside his brother.

"As if two injured sons were not enough," she complained, "there is now no wood for the fire."

Then Wally said, "I will go, mother. I will cut down a tree and bring wood for the fire."

"How could you succeed where your two brothers have failed?" said his mother scornfully.

"Why, you would cut off your own head," laughed his brothers.

"He may as well try," said his father. "If we lose him, it will be no great loss."

Grudgingly, his mother gave him some dough baked in the cinders and a jug of sour beer. But Wally was used to such treatment and made no complaint.

When he came to the forest, the old man was waiting. "Good sir," he said, "spare a little food for a hungry old man."

"I have only cinder bread and sour beer," said Wally, "but you are welcome to share it."

They sat down and he opened the basket and inside found cherry cake and sweet wine. Wally scratched his head in bewilderment. "Perhaps I picked up the wrong basket," he said, but in truth it was the old man's magic.

When they had eaten and drunk, the old man said, "Since you have a kind heart and share with those less fortunate, I will give you good luck. Cut down that old dead tree and see what you find beneath the roots."

Wally stared at the dead tree and then turned back to the old man . . . but he was nowhere to be seen. So he set to and chopped down the dead tree and the axe did not injure him at all. The old tree fell with a great crash and when the dust had cleared, he saw something gleaming among the roots. Peering down,

Wally found to his astonishment that it was a goose with feathers of pure gold. He picked it up and stroked its gleaming feathers with a gentle hand. Never in all his life had he possessed anything so beautiful.

If I go home, he thought, it will be taken away from me, for all the good things are given to my brothers. It seems then, that I must go out into the world and seek my fortune. With that he tucked the golden goose under his arm and set off through the forest.

All through the long day he walked and, as night fell, he reached the far edge of the forest and saw in the distance the lights of a little inn. I will rest for the night here, he thought, and pay my bill with a golden feather.

When the innkeeper saw the golden goose, he welcomed Wally with open arms, offering him good food and wine and his best bedroom. Poor Wally had never known such comfort and friendliness. When he had eaten his fill, he climbed into the comfortable bed and put the golden goose on the coverlet beside him. The goose settled herself to sleep, tucking her golden head beneath a golden wing. Wally lay with one arm around her, watching the gleam of moonlight upon her golden feathers until he fell asleep.

Now the innkeeper had three daughters and they had seen the golden goose.

When the youngest daughter went up to bed, she could hear Wally snoring peacefully in his room. If I could steal just one golden feather, she thought, I could buy myself a fine new bonnet. Cautiously, she opened the door and saw the golden goose sleeping in the moonlight. She tiptoed across the room and reached out her hand to pluck a feather. But the moment she touched the golden goose, her hand stuck fast to it and, try as she would, she could not pull it away.

The innkeeper's second daughter could not sleep. She kept thinking of Wally and his marvellous golden goose. If I had but a single feather, she thought, I could buy a pair of buckled shoes. She got up and stole quietly along the passage to the best bedroom. Peeping around the door, she saw that her younger sister was there before her.

"Sister! Sister!" she hissed. "What are you doing in a strange man's room?" She grasped the other girl and tried to pull her away from the bed, but at once her hand stuck fast to her sister's arm.

The third sister came up the stairs at that moment and, hearing whispered voices, went to find out the cause.

"Do not touch us, sister!" cried the younger two, as she put her head round the door.

"Touch you!" said the eldest sister angrily. "Why, I'll box your ears for you, you shameless hussies! Whispering in a stranger's room in the middle of the night!"

And before her sisters could stop her, she fetched the second sister a blow to the ear which left her hand glued to the side of the girl's head.

Now they found themselves in a sad confusion. Try as they might, they could not break free but were forced to pass the night in a heap on the bedroom floor. And through it all, Wally and the golden goose slept on peacefully.

When morning came and he found the innkeeper's three daughters stuck to each other and to his golden goose, Wally rubbed his eyes and thought hard.

"It seems, ladies," he said, "that you must come with me, for I am off to seek my fortune and must take the golden goose with me."

At this the three girls set up a terrible wailing, for they did not want to leave their home. Wally comforted them as best he could. "I doubt not," he said, "that in the great city we shall find some way to set you free." And with that he set out along the highroad carrying the golden goose under his arm, while the three girls ran awkwardly along behind him.

A few miles down the road, they passed a church. The parson, who was standing in the doorway, stared in dismay as the girls went by. He hurried after them calling: "Shame upon you! Is it seemly that three maids should chase a young man along a public highway?"

He seized the last sister by the arm to pull her back, but at once stuck fast and was towed along behind the others.

The sexton came out of the church and seeing the parson vanishing down the road, ran after him. "Your reverence," he cried. "Have you forgotten that we have a christening this morning?" He grabbed at the parson's sleeve, trying to attract his attention, but found himself caught in an instant and carried away like the rest.

Next they passed two farm labourers on their way to the fields and the parson called to them to rescue him and the sexton. They did their best, but no sooner had they seized hold of the sexton, than they found themselves held fast. There they were, all seven of them stuck to one another, trotting along behind Wally and his golden goose on the road to the big city.

Now it happened that the king of that land had only a single daughter and no sons. Both king and queen loved their child dearly and the hopes of all the kingdom lay in her wellbeing. When she was young she was a happy child, but as she came of an age to marry and princes came from far and wide to seek her hand, she fell into a deep melancholy.

She would not eat, and nothing that anyone could do would bring a smile to her face. Day by day she grew ever thinner and paler.

All the wise men and wise women of the kingdom came to see her, to try to find out the cause of her sadness, and all came away none the wiser.

At last they announced to the king that someone had put a spell upon his daughter. If the princess could only be made to smile, they declared, the spell would be broken and she would be well again. But if she remained in her deep sadness, they warned, the princess would waste away until she died.

The king and queen wept bitterly at the thought of losing their daughter. Then the king announced that whoever should made the princess smile, however lowly he might be, he should be free to seek her hand in marriage.

Young men arrived from all over the kingdom. Some told jokes, some juggled, some dressed up as clowns and did acrobatics: but the princess watched them all with an air of melancholy boredom. Daily she grew thinner and paler and her loving parents sank into despair.

It was at this point in our story that Wally reached the outskirts of the city. He looked so funny with his golden goose tucked underneath his arm and the three sisters, the parson, the sexton and the two labourers trotting behind, all at sixes and sevens, that the people in the streets began to laugh. Others who heard the laughter came running out from houses and shops and soon joined in. A crowd formed, all laughing together and began to follow behind him.

Wally was a cheerful soul and liked the sound of laughter. He smiled at the good people all around and began to laugh with them. As he marched on along the road, the crowd grew steadily larger and the laughter grew louder.

Then a bright lad in the crowd called out, "Let us take him to the palace! Surely our princess will smile when she sees him."

"Yes! Yes!" cried all the people and they led Wally and his little band towards the palace.

The princess was sitting sadly at her window, staring out into the palace yard. Slowly she became aware of a distant roaring sound that grew steadily louder. At first she could not make it out but as it drew closer it seemed to her very much like the sound of laughter.

Then suddenly Wally appeared around the corner and marched into the palace yard with the golden goose under his arm, the three sisters, the parson, the sexton and the two labourers stumbling along behind, and a great crowd of laughing people all round them.

Now laughter is quite as infectious as measles: even the sound of the crowd had begun to tickle the corners of the princess's mouth. The sight of Wally was too much for her. She broke into a loud peal of delighted laughter and once started found it hard to stop. When the king and queen came running in, breathless with hope, they found their beloved daughter leaning upon the window-sill, so helpless with laughter that she could hardly speak.

Delighted that the spell had at last been broken, the king and queen gave orders that Wally should be brought before them. He marched up the marble stairs, followed by his seven captives, and when he arrived in the room the princess, who had just managed to pause for breath, began laughing all over again.

The king and queen embraced Wally with tears of joy and gave their consent to the marriage if their daughter was willing.

Wally, who had quite fallen in love with the princess, knelt before her and set down his golden goose. At once the seven captives found themselves free.

Wally took the princess by the hand. "Will you marry me?" he asked her simply.

The princess smiled down at him. "If I do," she asked, "will you rule in my kingdom?"

Wally scratched his head and considered the matter. "I am a simple man, Your Highness," he said. "I fear I should not know how to rule a kingdom. But if you will have me, I will love you faithfully and do my best to be a good husband."

"Splendid!" said the princess. "Then I will marry you. All my other suitors wanted to be king: but it is my kingdom and I shall make an excellent queen."

And so it came about that Wally and the princess were married. When the ceremony took place Wally insisted on carrying the golden goose under his arm. "For then," he told the princess, "once our hands are joined, we can never be parted!"

SNOW WHITE

Once, on a winter's day, a queen sat sewing at her palace window. The window frame was made of ebony which showed black against the white snow beyond. As the queen stitched, she caught her finger on the needle and a drop of her red blood fell upon the snow. Then the queen thought to herself, I should like the child I bear to be a daughter as white as snow, as red as blood and as black as ebony.

Not long after, the queen was delivered of a baby girl and, just as she had wished, the child's skin was as white as snow, her lips red as blood and her hair as black and shining as ebony. The king and queen thought their daughter very beautiful and they called her Snow White. But the sweet queen who had longed for such a daughter fell ill and died soon after the child was born.

When a year had passed the king took himself a new bride, a woman of great beauty but proud and vain. This new queen was skilled in the art of magic and had a wondrous looking glass upon her wall. When she stood before this mirror and asked:

"Looking glass upon the wall,
Who is the fairest one of all?"

it would show in its depths whoever was most beautiful in the whole world. For many years the looking glass reflected always the queen's own lovely face and she was well pleased.

But, as her stepdaughter Snow White began to grow up, the girl grew even more beautiful, while the queen grew older and her beauty began to fade.

At last the day came when the queen faced her magic mirror and asked yet again:

"Looking glass upon the wall,
Who is the fairest one of all?"

and saw in its limpid depths the white skin, red lips and shining black hair of Snow White. Envy turned like a knife in the queen's heart, and from that hour she knew no peace, day or night, while Snow White lived.

At length, when the king, her husband, was away, the queen called her huntsman to her and said, "Take the girl, Snow White, into the forest and kill her. Bring me her heart as proof that the deed is done."

The huntsman obeyed and took Snow White deep into the forest far away from her home. There he seized hold of her and drew his knife to do the queen's bidding, but Snow White wept pitifully and begged the huntsman to spare her life.

"Lady," he said, "I dare not, for fear of the queen's anger."

"She need not know," said Snow White desperately. "I will go far away through the forest never to return."

She was so gentle and beautiful that the huntsman's heart was softened. He loosed his grip upon her and said: "Go quickly, then, before fear hardens my heart again." At once, Snow White fled into the depths of the forest.

The huntsman killed a wild boar and took its heart back to the queen, telling her that it was the heart of Snow White. The wicked queen looked at the heart and laughed and was for a while content.

Alone in the pathless forest, Snow White walked all day, through thorns and over sharp stones and as night fell, she grew faint with hunger.

Then, in a little grassy clearing, she came upon a tiny cottage and finding it empty and the door ajar, she went in to rest for a while. Inside she found a little room very neat and clean. On a white cloth on the table were set seven mugs and seven plates each with its knife, fork and spoon. Against the wall were seven little beds, each with a clean bright counterpane. Snow White ate a little of the bread which was on the table, and then lay down on one of the little beds.

I will only rest for a few moments, she thought, and be gone before the owners come home. But she was so tired after her long walk, that she fell fast asleep as soon as her dark head touched the soft pillow.

Now the cottage belonged to seven little dwarfs who worked all day at their mine in the mountains and returned at nightfall. When they came home, each carrying his little candle, they saw that some of their bread had been eaten.

"Who has been in our house?" they asked each other and, searching about, found Snow White lying asleep upon the bed. As the light of their candles fell upon her, they were astonished by her beauty. "It is some woodland nymph who honours our house," they whispered and were at pains not to wake her.

In the morning, when Snow White opened her eyes, she was at first afraid to see the seven strange little men around her. But they spoke to her kindly and, finding her to be no spirit but a homeless girl, asked how she came there. Snow White told them of her stepmother's cruelty and how she had been spared by the huntsman and had wandered far through the forest to reach their house.

When they had listened to her sad tale, the dwarfs talked for a while together and then said, "If you will cook for us and keep our little house while we work in the mines, you may live with us as long as you need shelter."

Snow White agreed most gratefully to this plan and for a while they all lived happily together. Snow White enjoyed caring for the little house which was now her home, and the dwarfs were happy to find a hot meal waiting when the long day's work was over. As time passed they grew very fond of their new housekeeper.

Now, for a long time Snow White's wicked stepmother did not trouble her magic looking glass. Believing that Snow White was dead, she never doubted that she was the most beautiful woman in the world. Until one day, having nothing better to do, she questioned the mirror idly, for the pleasure of seeing her own face reflected. But when she asked:

"Looking glass upon the wall,
Who is the fairest one of all?"

and gazed into the glass, she beheld the sweet face of the living Snow White, dishing out the evening meal in the seven dwarfs' cottage. The queen gave a great cry of rage and despair, for her rival was not only alive but had grown even lovelier than before.

Once more, the queen could not eat or sleep for the pangs of envy that racked her. By day and by night she could only think of some way to come at Snow White and harm her. She sent out spies to find where the seven dwarfs lived in the great forest. Then she disguised herself by her magic arts as an old pedlar woman and made her way to their house. She knocked at the door and cried, "See what pretty things I sell!"

Snow White came to the window and the pedlar woman set out her wares. "See my pretty silk laces," she said. "Here is a bright red one to lace up your bodice."

Now the lace of Snow White's bodice was indeed worn and frayed and she was glad to find a new one.

"Let me come in," said the old woman smiling, "and I will lace it up for you."

Trustingly Snow White let the old woman in and watched as, with deft fingers, she threaded the new lace and pulled it tight. Then she pulled it again and Snow White cried out: "No more, good soul! It is tight enough."

But the old woman laughed and pulled even tighter. Now Snow White could not cry out for want of breath, though she saw to her horror who the old woman was. But, even as she recognised the envious face of her stepmother, she fell to the floor and lay as if dead. The queen stared down at the lifeless body. "Now, I am the fairest," she said softly and she went away.

At night the seven dwarfs came home. Seeing their dear Snow White lying as if dead upon the floor, they cried out and knelt around her. There was a faint warmth still in her cheeks and seeing the new red lace, they quickly loosened it so that she could breathe again. When she was able to talk, Snow White told them of the queen's disguise. Then the seven dwarfs made her promise to lock the door when they were away and to let no one in.

Once more the wicked queen returned to her mirror and asked, never doubting the answer,

"Looking glass upon the wall,
Who is the fairest one of all?"

But again the mirror showed her the face of Snow White, sleeping peacefully now in her bed.

"What! Must it all be done again?" cried the queen angrily. "Then this time I shall not fail!"

Next day, she used her magic powers to fashion a deadly comb and, concealing herself in a new disguise, knocked once more at the door of the cottage.

"See my pretty trinkets, lady," she called.

Snow White did not forget her promise to let no one in. She opened the window a little and said, "I am sorry, good woman, but I must not open the door."

The old woman smiled cheerfully. "Quite right, my pretty," she said. "But it does no harm to look from your window." She held up a comb, very delicately made, and Snow White admired it. "It is cheap too," said the old woman. "Let me reach up and fix it in your lovely black hair."

Snow White leaned a little way out of the window and the old woman reached up to fasten the comb in her hair. But as she did so, she jabbed it sharply so that the poison should take effect. Snow White cried out and fell to the floor, where she lay without moving.

"What use is your black hair now?" cried the queen harshly and, gathering her dark cloak about her, she was gone into the forest.

When the seven dwarfs returned to find poor Snow White lying still and silent once more, they knew at once that it was the work of her stepmother. The comb gleamed in the blackness of Snow White's ebony hair and they quickly pulled it out. At once the girl began to stir and colour returned to her cheeks. Soon she could sit up, and told the dwarfs what had befallen.

"You must be ever on your guard," they told her. "Let no one in, buy nothing from anyone for fear of poison. " Snow White promised that she would be more careful.

When the queen came to her looking glass again she smiled in her triumph. Admiring the reflection of her own hard beauty, she demanded:

> "Looking glass upon the wall,
> Who is the fairest one of all?"

But the image did not hold: it grew pale and misty and when it cleared again, there was Snow White, sitting in a comfortable chair while the seven dwarfs fussed around her.

The queen screamed aloud, clenching her fist and stamping her feet in her anger. "I will destroy her now," she swore, "if it is the last thing I do . . . !"

She went to her most secret room at the top of a high tower, and there she made by her magic arts a poisoned apple. It was big and juicy and so cunningly made that only the red cheek contained the poison, while the green side was safe.

Next day, she disguised herself as a cheerful rosy-cheeked farmer's wife and went once more to the cottage. First she knocked at the door but Snow White did not answer. Then she looked in at the window and saw Snow White working busily. She tapped at the window-pane.

When Snow White saw the cheerful, friendly face she crossed to the window. "I am sorry," she said, "but I cannot let you in."

"Then open the window, my dear," said the farmer's wife. "I have fine apples to sell."

Snow White opened the window, just a little way and said, "I am not allowed to buy anything."

"No matter, my child," said the woman cheerfully. "See, I will give you one out of friendship."

"I cannot take it," said Snow White.

The farmer's wife looked hurt. "Why, goodness me!" she exclaimed. "Do you think I mean to poison you, my pretty?"

Snow White felt ashamed to be so unfriendly and the apple did look delicious.

"See," said the woman smiling. "I will eat half the apple and you shall eat the other half," and she bit into the green side of the apple.

It seemed churlish to go on refusing. Snow White smiled and, taking the apple, bit deeply into the other side.

At once the farmer's wife cried out in triumph and Snow White knew that she had been deceived. But it was too late: she had swallowed the apple and the poison did its deadly work. The last thing she heard was the queen's harsh voice, "White as snow, blood-red, black as ebony . . . but dead!" and her shrill laughter fading into the distance.

When the seven dwarfs found Snow White lying cold and lifeless, they were overcome with grief. They unlaced her, combed her hair and sought in vain to find some cause for her lifeless state. But they could find nothing nor could they bring her back to life.

Far off in her palace, the queen gazed into her magic looking glass and at last it showed her only her own cruel face.

The seven dwarfs laid Snow White's body upon a bier surrounded by leaves and flowers gathered from the forest around them. For three days they wept and kept watch around her. But when the day came for the burial, they saw that her cheeks were still rosy and that she looked for all the world as if she still lived. Then they could not bring themselves to lay her in the cold earth, but instead made a coffin of glass in which they laid her to rest. They set it up on the mountainside not far from the cottage, writing her name upon it in letters of gold, and always one of the dwarfs kept watch beside it.

And there, as autumn gave way to winter, Snow White lay in unchanging beauty: her skin like snow, her lips red as blood and her black hair shining like ebony.

One winter's day, a prince from a far kingdom was hunting in the forest, and came upon the glass coffin on the mountainside. He couldn't believe his eyes – he saw the beautiful maiden who lay inside and his heart was filled with love for her.

The dwarf who was keeping watch told him the sad story, and the young prince wept to think that he had found his love too late. He begged the dwarfs to

let him take the glass coffin back to his own kingdom, where he promised to build a fitting shrine for it. He offered to give them gold and jewels in return for it, but the seven dwarfs grew angry and told him that they would not part with Snow White for all the gold in the world.

"Then let me take the glass coffin as a gift," pleaded the prince. "My love is so great that, unless I can see Snow White, I shall die."

When they understood that his love was deep and true, the kindly dwarfs took pity on the prince and gave him leave to take the body of Snow White away with him.

The prince told his servants to lift the glass coffin on to their shoulders and to carry it with the greatest care. But the forest paths were rough and as they bore the coffin away, one of the men stumbled against the root of a tree. At once the piece of poisoned apple, which all this time had been lodged in Snow White's throat, was jolted free and she began to come back to life. A moment later she opened her eyes and found herself borne shoulder high in a box of glass. Puzzled, she lifted her hands to touch the glass and when the prince, who rode beside her, saw that she moved, his heart leaped with joy.

He told his servants to set her down upon the grass and at once released her from the coffin. Gazing at her in wonder, he saw that the living Snow White was lovelier than ever and he begged her to marry him.

At first she was confused, not knowing what had befallen her, until the dwarfs, learning that she still lived, came running to see the miracle. They told her all that had passed, and of the prince's great love for her. Then she smiled and gave him her hand and said that she would be his bride. Rejoicing, they set out for his father's kingdom where plans were soon made for a wedding of great splendour.

Now Snow White's father and her cruel stepmother were invited to the marriage feast, never knowing that the bride was their daughter. But when the wicked queen had put on her wedding finery she could not resist showing off her beauty before her magic mirror.

"Looking glass upon the wall,
Who is the fairest one of all?"

she asked, gazing with admiration at her own reflection. The mirror clouded and darkened, filling the queen's heart with an awful dread: when it cleared and brightened, she beheld her stepdaughter beautifully clothed in silk and jewels.

Snow White was laughing, holding the hand of her beloved prince, and her beauty dazzled the queen's eyes. She gave one terrible cry of rage and despair, and raising her fist, shattered the magic glass into a thousand pieces. And at that moment her heart, eaten away at last by envy and malice, ceased to beat and she fell dead among the splintered fragments.

But in the faraway kingdom, Snow White and her prince were married amid the rejoicing of all those who loved them, and they lived happily together all their days.

SWEET PORRIDGE

In a small village on the edge of a forest a little girl lived with her mother. She was a very good little girl, generous to her friends, kind to animals and helpful to old people. She was also very poor and often went hungry to bed.

One cold winter's day when she was in the forest gathering wood for the fire, she met an old woman bent on the same task.

"Ah! What it is to be young," said the old woman. "Your bundle of sticks is far bigger than mine, though I have been gathering all day. But my poor old hands are stiff and my back does not bend easily. Give me some of your wood, little girl, and you will not regret it."

"You can have it all, if you like," said the little girl. "I can soon find some more."

"You are very kind," said the old woman, "but I fear I could not carry so large a bundle."

"Then I will carry it home for you," said the little girl, for when she set out to help someone she was not easily put off.

So the good little girl took the bundle of sticks home for the old woman and it was well that she did. For the old woman was, in truth, a witch and might have turned her into a toad if she had refused to part with them As they went, the little girl told the witch all about herself and her mother and how very poor they were.

When they reached the witch's house and the bundle of sticks was safely stored, the old woman brought out a little iron pot.

"This is a magic porridge pot," she told the little girl, "and it will never fail you. Whenever you are hungry you have only to say, 'Cook, little pot,' and it will make sweet porridge for you.

When you have had enough you must say, 'Stop, little pot,' and it will stop.

But, remember, it will work only for you, because of your kindness, and no one else may use it."

The little girl thanked the old woman and hurried home to show the pot to her mother. She began to tell her what the witch had said and no sooner had she spoken the words, "Cook, little pot," than the iron pot began to bubble and plop! When they peeped inside, it was full of sweet creamy porridge.

Then their lives became very pleasant for, though they were still poor, they were never hungry, for they could always be certain of a hot meal at any time of the day.

Now, the little girl had told her mother that the pot would not work for anyone else, but one day when the little girl had gone to gather wood again, the mother grew hungry. It can do no harm to try, she thought and, making her voice as like her daughter's as she could, she said, "Cook, little pot." And the little pot was fooled by her piping voice and began to cook.

The mother was delighted. She filled her bowl from the pot again and again and, if the truth must be told, made quite a pig of herself. At last, when she could eat no more, she said, "Stop, little pot!" But by this time, she was so full that her voice sounded deep and breathless and not at all like the little girl's.

The little pot went on cooking. "Stop, little pot!" said the mother again, but the little pot was not to be fooled a second time.

The porridge bubbled up and suddenly poured over on to the table. The mother ran about, mopping at it with cloths, and all the time crying out, "Stop, little pot!" Sometimes she said it in a high voice and sometimes in a low voice, sometimes in a gruff voice and sometimes in a squeaky voice, but she never sounded in the least like the little girl.

Soon the porridge was running over the edge of the table and the mother tried to catch it in a bucket. Then it overflowed the bucket and began to spread across the floor.

"Oh! Whatever shall I do?" she cried. "Why did I not heed my daughter's warning?" The great tide of porridge drove her out through the door and began to spread across the garden. The mother ran to warn her neighbours.

"Foolish woman!" said the other wives, when they saw the mess and learned how it had come about. "You should have done as your good daughter told you!" They fetched their brooms and tried to sweep the porridge back as it crept into their gardens: but it only clogged up the bristles and kept on coming. As it crept up the paths to their doors, the neighbours were driven back into their houses. Locking their doors and fastening their windows, they watched in dismay as the porridge ran up the walls outside. The light grew dim as it covered the windows.

Meanwhile the mother had run up the hillside and into the forest in search of her daughter. The good little girl, who was patiently gathering her sticks, heard her mother's voice calling through the trees: "Daughter! Daughter! Come quickly before the whole village is drowned in porridge!"

"Oh, mother!" said the good little girl. "What *have* you done!"

"I meant no harm," said her mother tearfully. "I was hungry and the little pot was so tempting. Only stop the porridge and I will never, never do it again!"

They ran to the edge of the forest and saw that the porridge had spread into a great lake with only the roofs and chimneys of the village to be seen.

Without wasting a moment, the little girl cried, "Stop, little pot!" as loudly as she could and deep down beneath the porridge, the magic pot heard her. At once it stopped and the village was saved.

The mother had learned her lesson and in future always did as her daughter said. But as for the porridge! Well, the people in the houses had to eat their way out; and those who were out working in the forest and field had to eat their way back in; and it was a long time before any of them could face a porridge pot again.

THE ELVES AND THE SHOEMAKER

There was once an old shoemaker, a good and honest man, who fell ill and could work no more. He had a loving wife to care for him but, as he could not earn his living, they grew very poor. In time the wife nursed her husband back to health again and he felt strong enough to work. But by this time they were so poor that he could afford leather for only one pair of shoes. Very carefully the shoemaker cut out the shoes and set them on his workbench.

"That is enough for one day," said his wife, for with the poor food which was all they could afford, the old man soon grew tired. "Leave the stitching until the morning," she said gently. "Your eyes are tired and the light is poor, and if you spoil your work, we have no more leather."

"You are wise," said the shoemaker. "I will do as you say." He left the shoes upon the bench and the good couple said their prayers and went to bed.

But in the morning when the old man came to his work, he found the shoes already finished. He called his wife, and they stared at the shoes in astonishment. "See how fine they are," said the shoemaker, "with tiny stitches such as my old hands could never do!"

"We are blessed, indeed!" exclaimed his wife and, being a practical person, she added, "Put them in the window quickly, that they may find a buyer."

It was not long before a customer came who greatly admired the workmanship and paid a high price for the shoes.

"Now," said the shoemaker, "I can afford enough leather for two pairs of shoes."

Once again he cut them out with care, and once again his wife made him set them aside until morning. Next day the old couple woke early feeling that their luck had turned at last. And when the shoemaker came to his bench, there stood two pairs of shoes, finished as neatly as the first. These found willing buyers, and the shoemaker was able to buy leather for four pairs of shoes. Again, in the morning, all four pairs were made, and the next day eight pairs.

Now the old woman could buy good food and the old man grew strong again. His hands grew steady so that in a day he could cut out many pairs of shoes. But however many pairs there were, and whatever style or fashion, whether for man, woman or child, always in the morning the shoes were perfectly made. Before the year was out, the old couple had grown quite wealthy and knew that whatever the future might hold, they would never be poor again.

Now in all this time, the shoemaker and his wife had never sought to know how their good fortune had come about. It seemed to them only as the answer to their prayers. Then, one evening, when it was nearly Christmas, the old man said to his wife, "I have a mind to keep watch tonight and see who it is that helps us, for we take always and give nothing in return."

"You are right, my dear," said his wife. "And I will keep you company." She lit a lamp and left it burning while she and her husband hid behind some old clothes which hung in the corner of the room.

For a long time nothing happened. The old couple dozed a little and had to keep waking each other up. Then, at last, when the lamp was beginning to burn low, and the sound of the midnight chimes drifted over the sleeping town, they heard the faint creak of the door opening. The old woman caught hold of her husband's hand and held her breath.

Into the room and on to the workbench came two little elves. Setting to work at once they stitched and hammered, working so quickly and so skilfully, that before long all the shoes were done. Then they set the pairs out in rows, surveyed their handiwork with some pride, and jumping swiftly to the floor, ran over to the door. For a moment the wind whined in the doorway: then the door closed with a creak and the little elves were gone.

The shoemaker and his wife were so astonished they could hardly believe what they had seen. "We will sleep upon it," said the wife, "and resolve in the morning what we should do."

When the new day came, the old shoemaker wondered if they had fallen asleep during the long waiting and perhaps dreamed the whole thing.

"And yet the shoes are always made," said his wife. "Someone must be making them."

"It is certain that they have made us rich," said the old man. "We must find some way to thank them."

They pondered the matter for some time, thinking first of one gift, then another, but nothing seemed quite right for the little elves. Until suddenly the wife said, "I have it, husband! It seemed to me that the little creatures were not properly dressed for the cold winter weather outside. I will make them little shirts and coats and trousers; I will knit them woollen hats and socks and little gloves; and you must make each one a tiny pair of leather shoes."

"A splendid idea!" cried the old man. "My hands are now steady enough to do it."

They worked long and hard, taking great pleasure in their secret tasks, and at last the little clothes were made and the tiny shoes completed.

On the night before Christmas, they hung the house with holly and ivy and, instead of the cut leather for the shoes, set out their gifts upon the workbench.

Then they hid themselves again to see what the little elves would make of them.

On the stroke of midnight the door creaked open, letting in a quick flurry of snow. The little elves came hurrying in, hunching their shoulders against the cold. For a few moments they warmed themselves by the heat of the lamp, to thaw their cold fingers for the task ahead. Then they turned to begin their work and seemed puzzled to find no shoes cut out. When they saw, instead, the little clothes, so daintily and cleverly fashioned, they were at first surprised and then delighted.

Laughing, they put on the beautiful clothes and the tiny shoes, holding up each new item to admire it. When they were dressed they danced about, preening themselves and admiring one another. As they pulled on their woollen hats and their warm gloves they sang:

"Now we are so fine to see,
Why should we two cobblers be?"

And, still singing, they danced right out of the door into the Christmas night, leaving behind a trail of tiny footprints in the fallen snow.

The old couple never saw them again. But as the old man said: "A shoemaker who could make shoes for elves would never want for money." And so it was: to the end of their lives the old couple lived in good health and happiness and prospered in all they did.